CW01189726

Harry
and the Lost Sheep

By Ruth Chesney

Illustrated by Mary Weatherup

RITCHIE
John Ritchie Publishing

40 Beansburn, Kilmarnock, Scotland

ISBN-13: 978 1 912522 34 7

Copyright © 2018 by John Ritchie Ltd.
40 Beansburn, Kilmarnock, Scotland

www.ritchiechristianmedia.co.uk

Scripture quotations marked "NKJV" are taken from the New King James Version®. Copyright© by Thomas Nelson, Inc. Used by permission. All rights reserved.

All rights reserved. No part of this publication may be reproduced, stored in a retrievable system, or transmitted in any form or by any other means – electronic, mechanical, photocopy, recording or otherwise – without prior permission of the copyright owner.

Typeset by John Ritchie Ltd., Kilmarnock
Printed by Bell & Bain, Glasgow

This is Harry.

Harry lives on a farm with Daddy, Mummy, Little Sister Susie and Toby the dog.

One day Harry helped Daddy to count the sheep.

One…two…three…

…all the way up to ninety-nine.

Daddy pulled off his cap and scratched his head.

"There should be one hundred," he said. "One is lost! We'd better go and find it."

So Daddy and Harry set off to find the lost sheep.

They peeked into the cowshed, but there were only cows there, resting and munching their hay.

"Moooo!" said Matilda the cow.

They tried the hayshed.

Marmalade the cat was sleeping on the bales…

…but the sheep wasn't there.

They walked down the lane...  ...climbed over a gate...

...and up a steep, grassy hill.  Harry's legs were very tired.

They clambered over a stone wall and crossed a wet, squelchy field.

"Where are you, Sheep?" called Harry.

"Ruff ruff," barked Toby the dog.

Daddy helped Harry to cross a bubbling little stream.

They looked into a muddy ditch.

No sheep!

They squeezed through a gap in a prickly hedge.

Toby the dog pricked up his ears.

Harry listened too. Baaa!

Toby and Harry ran towards the sound…

…and there was the lost sheep! She was all tangled up in long, thorny briars and couldn't get free.

Daddy pulled at the thorns. They were sharp; they cut his hands.

The sheep was very tired. She had been there for a long, long time.

Daddy put her on his shoulders and carried her. When Harry got tired, Daddy carried him as well. Daddy is very strong!

As soon as they got home, Harry ran to the house. "Mummy! We found the lost sheep!"

Mummy gave Harry a big hug. "The Lord Jesus told a story about a lost sheep," she said. "The shepherd went a long way to find it, and when he brought it home his friends and neighbours were really happy!"

(Luke 15:3-7)

"Sheep get lost because they want to go their own way and go places where they shouldn't go. We have all done bad things which God says we shouldn't do. So we are just like sheep because we want to go our own way instead of God's way. We deserve to be punished."

(Isaiah 53:6)

"The shepherd is like the Lord Jesus. He came all the way from Heaven to rescue us. He was put on a cross and He died to take the punishment instead of us."

"That's like the verse I learned in Sunday school," said Harry. "Jesus said, 'I am the good shepherd. The good shepherd gives His life for the sheep.' "

(John 10:11)

"That's right," smiled Mummy. "And if we trust in Him we are saved and won't be punished. When we get saved, even the angels are happy because we have been rescued."

"Now, how about some milk and biscuits for this little shepherd?"